ALIENS

The Perfect Cover

James C. Reinhold

Contents

Dedication

To all those who would believe without seeing, know that Science Fiction could one day be Science fact, and never be afraid to use their Imagination.

Acknowledgment

To my wife, children, family, friends, and teachers who kept me believing.

About the Author

Greetings,

I am James C. Reinhold, Author, and Holder of Https://readtorelax.com

I happily retired after 30 years of service doing something I loved doing. My passion now is to write engaging, science fiction, fantasy, and religious stories. I enjoy writing, as I am a new and enthusiastic author with a vision for fiction. My hope is to have my stories earn readers. This time, I have decided to collect all my work in one place, and let your imagination select your journey. Fantasy, Fiction, and Religion are my genres at present.

Books Driven by Passion

Reading is a personal journey. Bookmark your next reading journey with us at Https://www.readtorelax.com Select books that embrace your imagination at our cozy site and experience reading like you are in the story. All my books are Journeys that hopefully never lose your interest as readers, each of my books will embrace your imagination, from visiting Christmas 1967 to traveling through wormholes. As you start to read my books, you feel gripped by the storyline. Before putting my thoughts to the pen, I consider the story from every aspect to ensure that my readers have something interesting to read, like suddenly hearing that favorite song that just came on the radio, Turn it Up!

A Book for Every Taste

All my books are available as e-books, paperback, and hardcover from Amazon, Barnes and Noble, Https://www.readtorelax.com and our Audible audiobooks are available from Amazon, iTunes, and Barnes and Noble.

CHAPTER 1

Have you ever found yourself clutching onto a precious secret so tightly, as if it were the only thing keeping you afloat in a sea of chaos? The kind of secret that feels like a weight on your chest, begging to be shared with someone you trust. You turn to your dearest friend, and with a voice trembling with both fear and excitement, you utter those sacred words: "I need to tell you something, but you cannot breathe a word of it to anyone."

At that moment, you are placing your life in their hands. It's a gamble, a risk that could cost you everything you hold dear. Yet, the temptation to release this heavy burden is simply too great. Because what if this secret was a matter of life and death? What if it wasn't just your own life at stake but that of your confidante too? The stakes are high, the risks are real, and the consequences are dire. But for a moment, you feel alive with the thrill of having shared your secret with another soul.

Listen closely, my dear friend, for I am about to divulge a secret that will shake you to your very core. Brace yourself, for what I am about to reveal is nothing short of a phenomenon that defies all reason and logic. Yes, it's true. I am privy to one of the biggest, craziest secrets about our country that you could ever imagine. It's the kind of secret that will leave you gasping for breath, questioning everything you thought you knew about our nation. The kind of secret that makes your heart race with excitement and anticipation while at the same time filling you with dread and uncertainty. And yet, despite the enormity of this revelation, I cannot keep it to myself any longer. For the world must know the truth about our country, even if it means putting my own safety at risk. So, are you ready to hear the truth?

For decades there has been a buzz about the information I have known for years, from Presidents, armed forces, and civilians, but no one could confirm any information on this phenomenon. You will find out why later in these notes. If I thought that the information was harmful to the USA, I would try to divulge it, but it would not be easy. I think it would do more damage than good.

Every time there was a news clip or a live real-time scene, or even a documentary on this phenomenon, I would just smile, knowing that I knew the real story. If I started a conversation with the most trusted person I knew about my secret, they would look at me as if I was a mental patient.

It's a daunting thought, isn't it? To entrust someone with a secret so precious, so delicate, that it could change the course of your life forever. But what happens when the person you turn to for comfort and support, the one you consider your most trusted confidante, meets your revelation with a look of incredulity? A look that suggests they believe you to be a raving lunatic spewing forth the mad ramblings

2

of a deranged mind. It's a chilling realization, to be sure. For in that moment, you are not only stripped of your courage but also of your sense of belonging. Suddenly, you feel like an outsider, an outcast, an individual whose thoughts and beliefs are too radical, too unconventional, for the world to accept. And yet, the secret still lingers a heavy burden on your soul, begging to be released. Will you find the strength to continue, to seek out a true ally who will listen with open ears and an open heart? Or will you succumb to the fear of being deemed a mental patient and keep your secret locked away forever? The choice is yours, my friend.

So why am I talking now? Well, because these notes are part of my will if you are reading this, I have carried this burden with me to my death, and I am giving this information to a select few people, and they can decide what to do with it. My job is in a seclusive Branch of the US Government, which leads me to meet all interesting people with fascinating backgrounds, and this includes my friend, Bill.

Bill and I seemed to connect with each other upon our first meeting, and through the years, we agreed on a ton of ideas and talked out our differences. I swore he was a Road Scholar; you could mention any conversation from baseball to nanotechnology, and Bill would hold an intense conversation about the subject. Little did I know our friendship would change my ideas about life and America forever.

Bill was a man of two worlds, each one as fascinating and complex as the other. On the one hand, he was drawn to the mysteries and possibilities of outer space, constantly seeking out information and insights from the brightest minds at NASA. On the other hand, he had an equally intense passion for the earth beneath his feet, dedicating hours upon hours to studying the intricacies of agriculture and the latest trends emerging from the Department of Agriculture. It was a strange dichotomy, to be sure, but one that made Bill even more captivating to those around him. He was a sponge for knowledge, soaking up every detail and tidbit he could get his hands on. And yet, for all his intelligence and curiosity, he remained an enigma when it came to his personal life. Even to me, who was his closest friend, his confidant—he was tight-lipped and guarded, revealing only glimpses of his innermost thoughts and feelings. It was a tantalizing mystery, one that kept his acquaintances and colleagues on their toes, always eager to learn more about this fascinating man who seemed to have a universe of secrets locked away inside him.

His mantra, since I had known him, was "Seeds in Space." He was constantly pushing our Space program to evaluate the ability of seeds in space, seed germination, metabolism, genetics, biochemistry, and even seed production, constantly trying to promote and push space biology. Of course, we all knew that if we inhabited another Earth-like planet, we would need to feed our population, and it was a noble project, but as I grew to know Bill, the future of Earth's population was not his intention, it was the Earth itself.

As I have said before, I was in a Catch22. What I knew was not in any way harming Earth. While I was friends with Bill and his "Family," I only saw Earth benefiting from their group knowledge, but could I guarantee it in the future? The answer to that was "No."

Imagine a world where the truth could bring down entire governments, incite global panic, and threaten the very fabric of our society. A world where secrets are not only kept but fiercely protected, even at the cost of our own safety. This is the world that I live in, a world where I cannot even utter the names of the people, I know for fear of what might happen if that knowledge falls into the wrong hands. Instead, I must address them by first name only, a measure of caution that seems trivial but could mean the difference between life and death. You see, these people are part of a "family" - a complex, shadowy organization that operates in the shadows, unknown to most of the world. And while some members of this family have been a boon to our national security, there are others whose motives are far more sinister. I cannot predict what the future holds or how far this family's reach extends beyond our borders. All I can do is hold tight to what little information I have and pray that I am never forced to reveal the full extent of what I know.

CHAPTER 2

For Bill, there was no greater joy than the simple act of walking. It was a hobby, a love, a source of peace and tranquility in a world that was often chaotic and overwhelming. And when it came to walking, there was no better place to be than in the park - surrounded by the lush greenery, the sound of birds singing, and the fresh scent of nature filling his lungs. After a long day at work, Bill would make his way to the park, letting his feet carry him wherever they pleased. Sometimes he would wander down the well-worn paths, lost in thought and reflection. Other times he would venture off the beaten track, exploring the hidden corners of the park that few people ever saw. And as the sun began to set and the sky turned a deep shade of orange and purple, Bill made his way back home, feeling renewed and refreshed by his time in the park. It was a ritual that he cherished, a precious moment of peace in a world that was often so hectic and demanding.

One day I was lucky enough to finish work at the same time as Bill and decided to share the walk with him. The weather was beautiful and cool for a walk. My heart was racing as I darted through the park, my eyes scanning the trees and foliage for any sign of movement. And then, there he was - ahead of me, walking off the beaten path, disappearing into the shadows. I slowed my pace, trying to keep a low profile as I followed him, watching his every move. Had he seen me? Did he suspect anything? I could not be sure. But as he disappeared out of sight, I felt a sense of relief wash over me. Maybe I had caught a break. But as the minutes ticked by and he failed to reappear, my relief turned to worry.

"What was taking him so long? Had he stumbled into trouble?" I thought to myself.

With my heart pounding in my chest, I retraced his steps, following the sound of a faint buzzing that grew louder with each passing moment. And then, in the darkness, I saw a figure.

"Was it him? Or something else entirely?" I could not make it out, but my instincts told me to approach with caution. The park was always a peaceful place, but at that moment, anything could happen.

"Bill," I spoke laughingly, "are you back here?"

My heart was pounding in my chest as I stumbled through the park, my eyes wide with fear. And then, out of nowhere, a bright red light pierced through the darkness, glowing like a beacon from high up in the trees. At first, I thought it was just a trick of the light, a figment of my imagination. But as I looked up, I saw it—a face, not human, not anything I had ever seen before. Two glowing red eyes stared down at me, a face that seemed to shift and move as if alive. I wanted to run, to flee for my life, but my legs would not move. I was rooted to the spot, frozen in terror. It felt like an eternity before I could move again, my body trembling with fear as I stumbled backward and fell to the ground. As I picked myself up and started to run, I knew I had to get away—as far away as possible. I ran faster than I ever had before, the panic and fear driving me on. People around me looked on in confusion as I hurtled past them, my eyes wild with terror. I couldn't stop. I couldn't slow down—not until I was sure I was safe. But even then, I could not shake the memory of that glowing, alien face haunting me with every step.

"What did I just see? How could I imagine such an alien figure? Whether I imagined it or not? Where was Bill? Did he need help?" I asked too many questions, all at a time to myself.

Desperate for an answer, I knew what I had to do. I had to go back and figure it all out. I could not leave my friend there. Walking back to the original spot, I could see a figure walking toward me. It was Bill.

I walked a little faster to reach him and asked, "Are you alright?"

"Yes," Bill replied. "What are you doing in the park?" he asked instantly.

I told him I wanted to share a walk with him, so I hurried to catch up until I saw him walking off the path.

"I waited for you, and fifteen minutes had lapsed," I told him. "I continued finding you, thinking something was wrong. Do not tell me you did not see that 'Thing' that was in the tree?"

"Yes," replied Bill, "I did see something. What was it?"

"I have no idea," I whispered, "but I think I should report it."

"Let's sit and relax," Bill answered. "You look frazzled."

It was then my life changed, and one of our biggest questions in life made sense now. ARE ALIEN SIGHTINGS REAL?

"What if I told you that 'thing' in the tree was me?" He said with utter seriousness.

I began laughing so hard I was choking on my water.

"Thanks for calming me down with your humor Bill," I said while wiping my face. I looked back at Bill, and he looked as serious as I had ever seen him. "What in Sam Hill are you talking about?" I almost yelled.

Bill's eyes sparkled with excitement as he leaned forward and spoke in hushed tones, his words carrying the weight of a mind-blowing revelation. "Picture a civilization of beings that are born with the power of the atom at their fingertips, having harnessed it through millions of years of evolution in the darkest, emptiest reaches of space. These beings, these flying power grids, are a true force to be reckoned with. And they are out there, somewhere, waiting for us to discover them."

Bill spoke with excitement in his voice, his eyes sparkling with the thrill of the unknown. He leaned in closer, as if sharing a secret, and began to describe a civilization that seemed too fantastical to be true. His tale of flying power grids and creatures that were part bee, part human, with a society that valued the importance of plant life. As he spoke, it was clear that he believed every word and that he had discovered something truly remarkable. His words painted a picture of a world beyond our wildest imaginations, a world that we could only dream of exploring.

"Bee-like human creatures," he continued, "or you can say Bee Centaurs. These bee-like creatures are more than just insects. They are highly intelligent and able to communicate with each other in a language all their own. Their goal is to create a better future for their offspring, and to achieve this, they harness the power of evolution over millions of years. Living on the planet Pherzon, they coexist with a diverse population of other Centaurs, all with their unique blend of human and animal features. And with their complex diet, the Bee Centaurs requires much more than just the nectar of flowers to sustain them."

As he spoke, I could hardly believe my ears. Bill was describing a civilization of beings that were part human, part insect, and all bees. They communicated with each other and had a deep desire to improve the lives of future generations by finding more sources of sustenance. These Bee Centaurs

11

had been ruling the planet Pherzon for millions of years, along with a variety of other Centaur species that also called it home. With their unique biology, they needed a significant amount of food to survive - more than just insects and bees. It was like something out of a science fiction novel, yet he spoke with such conviction that I found myself fascinated by his words.

"Bill, wait," I said, interrupting him. "What are you talking about? Why are you playing with me?"

"I am serious," he replied.

"I saw what looked to be an alien back there. Are you not listening?"

Bill continued as if I was not even talking. "I am telling you this story because you are my closest and only loyal friend that I can trust. This is not a science fiction story. This is as real-time as it gets, and I am just asking for you to hear me out."

"I'm all ears," I responded with a questionable smile, humoring his request.

As Bill continued his story, my mind struggled to keep up with the fantastical world he was describing. It was as if he had opened a portal to a realm beyond human comprehension, one where Bee-like creatures reigned supreme and harnessed the power of the atom through their very birth. But as much as I found his tale hard to believe, I could not help but be drawn in by his conviction and enthusiasm. It was as if he honestly believed every word he was saying, and for a moment, I wondered if he knew something the rest of us didn't.

CHAPTER 3

As I listened to Bill, I began to ponder if what he was saying could be true. On the other hand, I couldn't help but think that Bill might know more than any of us.

I focused my attention as he continued, "My planet, Pherzon, was a planet unlike Earth, but it evolved over millions of years just like Earth did. Its location adapted and survived through time with its own environment and evolution. The evolution of Pherzon adapted to its environment for as long as Earth's did. Pherzon was located so far into space that neither Earth nor Pherzon knew of each other until Pherzon sent out scouts. In the early 1900s, the Bee Centaurs started sending out their Bee Drones to explore the cosmos for a habitat with abundant food. After decades of searching, the drones eventually discovered Planet Earth. Most Bee Drones would perish during the mission because giving up was not an option when ordered by the Queen. The drones flew in pairs, with a larger Bee Centaur carrying a smaller one on its back. The passenger would hopefully make it back from the journey by resting on the back of the traveler. In late 1940, they found Planet Earth, and the passenger drone returned to Pherzon to inform the Queen Bee of the discovery."

As Bill continued speaking, I sat there, completely stunned by what he was revealing. These Bee centaurs were a remarkable species with incredible powers of flight and shapeshifting, honed through generations of evolution. Their ability to morph into any form and fly with stealth or visibility was truly remarkable. In the darkness, they could harness the power of light energy to become a glowing form, and over time, their powers only grew stronger from their missions, giving them an impressive level of stamina. After discovering Earth, the Queen Centaur had watched the planet for generations and, in the late 1940s, devised a plan to send her workers and drones to Morph in human form and transport themselves to strategic positions on Earth, such as governmental and scientific positions which in the future, would help their own planet, Pherzon. While on Earth, they would slowly gather locations and give themselves an impeccable fake identity which would include information from the best schools, colleges, and life challenges. The centaurs had a superior mind. They could absorb any language, including Earth's computer language. They were like chameleons and could fit into any situation and not be awkward. They studied Earth for generations and built Algorithms in their minds for any situation.

I could not help but feel a sense of disbelief as Bill continued his incredible story. "How was I supposed to keep a straight face through all of this?" My mind was reeling with questions and doubts, yet I couldn't help but feel a spark of curiosity. "What if what Bill was saying was true?" The idea of morphing Bee Centaurs and their advanced abilities was something straight out of a science fiction novel, but the manner Bill spoke with such conviction made me wonder if there was some truth to his words. I tried to focus on his story, hoping to glean some sort of insight or explanation for this unbelievable tale.

As Bill continued to spin his tale, I could not help but wonder if he had completely lost his mind. But despite my skepticism, I listened intently as he elaborated on the Bee Centaur's plan to infiltrate Earth's society.

"Their mindset," Bill explained, "was to slowly occupy every significant role on Earth in time, and that would give their civilization control if they ever needed it. They did not want to defeat or 'take over' Earth, they wanted to live their lives to their benefit without Earth knowing they were there, and so far, it is working."

I could not believe what I was hearing. The idea that an alien race was covertly taking over Earth was absurd, but Bill seemed convinced.

"Their positions on Earth would benefit Earth because of their superior knowledge, decision-making, and their leadership qualities," Bill continued, "but make no mistake, the main reason for occupying Earth was for the survival of their own planet, Pherzon."

I couldn't help but roll my eyes at the idea of aliens using humans for their own benefit. But despite my disbelief, I could not deny that Bill's story was strangely compelling. There was more to this than I thought…

He continued, "When you witnessed me in the tree, I was taking honey from a beehive. Your Earth bees sense I am a Queen Bee and allow me to remove what I want. Of course, I would not starve their Queen or others. A Queen Bee-Centaur, which is who I am, has a combative glow when approached, as do my drone and helper centaurs. A defense mechanism, a built-in scare tactic that freezes our enemy for just a second, and that is enough time for the Centaur to assume stealth or remove itself from harm to a location of safety. When I am in flight with my drones and worker centaurs, we can move from zero to hyper speed in the blink of an eye. If we are in flight formation and are in path with anything, our defense light glows, and in milliseconds we are gone. Every Earth sighting of us in the air is our glow and then darkness, which Earth has categorized as a UFO sighting. Every land sighting of us is the glow of our face and then darkness, which Earth has depicted as a human form with an elongated head and eyes, which you have categorized as an Alien, which is what you had seen in the park. What the sightings miss is our entire Bee head, wings, and human-like body, which does not glow. This has been our mystique on earth and how we fit in so well. Our Earth centaurs will go out at night for food in Centaur form, most likely in parks, forests, and farms. Most of your UAP, UFO, or Alien sightings are at this time when they see the combative glow from our Bee's head, it benefits us since we are able to disappear, and it lists another Alien sighting which disguises us since it is so intriguing to Earth humans and Media. Your government has so many sightings of us they have started its own Unidentified Aerial Phenomena Task Force, which is a program within the United States Office of Naval Intelligence used to "standardize the collection and reporting" on sightings of unidentified aerial phenomena, sometimes termed UFOs."

I looked at Bill as if he had two heads, not a bee's head. His story about the Bee Centaurs from planet Pherzon occupying Earth in disguise was getting increasingly absurd.

"Okay," I slurred, trying to sound polite, "I think I should be heading home now."

I couldn't help feeling uneasy around Bill, wondering if he had some sort of mental illness that I wasn't aware of. I needed to get away from him and his bizarre stories.

"See you tomorrow," I said.

Bill replied, "Okay."

As I rose from the bench to clear my head, my body suddenly went limp, and I collapsed back onto the seat. There, in front of me, was the same alien face that I had seen in the tree. As I regained my senses, I glanced over, and the image turned back into Bill's face, sitting next to me with a smile on his face.

"This needs to be our secret, my friend," he said quietly while smiling. "I know it's a lot to take in," Bill said sympathetically. "But it's the truth, and you need to keep it a secret. If anyone finds out, it could be dangerous for both of us."

"I won't breathe a word of this to anyone, Bill," I promised with a shaky voice. "But I have to admit, this is a lot to take in. I appreciate you confiding in me, and I'm sorry for following you to the park. This whole situation is going to be strange tomorrow, but I'll have plenty of questions for you."

Bill nodded, a serious look on his face. "I understand, and I'm glad you're taking this seriously. It's important that we keep this between us for now."

"But what am I supposed to do now? How do I go back to my normal life after this?"

Bill patted my shoulder reassuringly. "We'll figure it out," he said. "Just try to act normal, and we'll talk more tomorrow."

As we walked home, I could not shake the feeling that I had stumbled into some kind of top-secret government operation. But this was even more bizarre—an alien civilization that had infiltrated Earth, all without our knowledge. My mind raced with questions and doubts. "Was Bill telling the truth? Was I just a pawn in some secret intergalactic plan? And why was he so insistent on me keeping quiet about it all?"

As we reached my apartment building, I thanked Bill for walking me home and went inside, feeling both relieved and unsettled. Little did I know that Bill was still outside, watching my every move, waiting to see if he could trust me with the most extraordinary secret of all.

As I lay in bed that night, my mind racing with questions, I realized that my life would never be the same. I had stumbled upon a secret that could change the course of human history—if only I could figure out what to do with it.

CHAPTER 4

The next few days were agonizing for me. I had to confront Bill about his unbelievable story, but I didn't know where to start. Should I function as if nothing had happened and just try to find the underlying cause of things on my own? That is exactly what I decided to do. The truth was that Bill's story about the Centaurs on Earth had me hooked.

Eager to learn about UFO and Alien sightings, I started to investigate all past sightings. I spent hours researching and looking into past sightings, and to my amazement, I was able to connect them all to Bill's story. It was like putting together pieces of a puzzle, and everything fit perfectly. I could not believe what I had uncovered. It was the greatest story ever told, and I was the only one who knew about it. Every time there was another "alien" sighting, my excitement grew. I knew the real reason behind it, and it gave me chills. No one knew any better, and it fits so perfectly with the excitement every time there was another "Alien" sighting. Even better than that, every Alien or UFO sighting there was, I knew the reason behind it. I was keeping the greatest story ever told, but how long could I keep this secret? But with great power comes great responsibility. I couldn't keep this secret forever. I needed to talk to Bill and find out everything. Who else knows about this? How long have they been here? When will they leave? And most importantly, are humans in danger?

I needed to talk to Bill to find out why, how long, and who else knew when they would leave. Humans are in danger. My head was spinning, and it was showing in my work.

Days turned into a week, and I still had not talked to Bill about his unbelievable story. But it was consuming my every thought. I spent my days investigating and connecting the dots, and my nights were spent wondering how I could keep this secret forever.

But then, out of nowhere, Bill approached me. "Hey, wanna walk through the park tonight?" he asked.

I hesitated for a moment. Was this a clever idea? What if he had changed his mind and decided that I couldn't be trusted? What if I became a missing person after this meeting with Bill?

But my curiosity got the best of me, and I agreed to meet him. Well, that was the longest workday of my life. If I were still his friend, I could not wait to hear the story behind the story. It was a long day, but we finally called it and started heading to the park. As we walked through the park, I couldn't help but feel like I was walking into the unknown. We sat at a bench where not too many pedestrians passed by. I was eager to start my questions.

After a few minutes of small talk, Bill finally spoke. "I know you've been investigating my story," he said, his eyes piercing into mine.

I froze. "How did he know? Did he find out about my research?"

"It's okay," he continued. "I've been expecting it. I just need to know if I can trust you."

I took a deep breath and gathered my thoughts. "Yes, you can trust me," I said confidently. "But I need to know everything. Why are they here? How long have they been here? And most importantly, are humans in danger?"

Bill sighed heavily. "It's a long story," he said. "But I promise to tell you everything."

"Bill, I'm eager to hear your story," I said confidently.

"Then let me tell my story, and if you have any questions, we will talk them out," he said to which I completely agreed.

"I will start with my planet, Pherzon. Our location is in Dark Space; our planet and living conditions would be comparable to Earth before humans. Think of a planet with all plants and animals or plants and centaurs. We are a peaceful planet with a hierarchy and a circle of life, your "President" on Earth would be me on Pherzon, the Prime Queen Bee, and as your President is, the Queen is replaced annually for varied reasons. On our planet, the prime queen bee is the Queen of the planet, no one can come close to her power, and no one would ever challenge her. Her drone and worker bee centaurs would protect her with their lives. Through generations of queen bees, we grew with more power, able to kill in a second's time, able to fly at warp speed if needed, able to transport to any form she needed, anywhere, anytime. She had the power of twenty centaurs and the mindset to gather all information. She was nothing short of an enigma. The Prime Queen Centaur was well respected and feared, but she always put her planet and centaurs first. I look to Earth as a prospect for abundant food for my planet. We have no manufacturing or modern farming tools or techniques. Our planet does have space and water and does have light from stars and quasars. Our trees and plants were always abundant, but with every planet, we now have a population problem. Not only that but through generations, our multitude of Centaurs has grown larger and stronger. We are a family-friendly planet, and anyone who abuses the family and what it stands for is subject to stand before the Queen Centaur. We are very respectful of our environment, but we need replenishment faster than natural growth. As for myself, being half Bee, half-human, my centaurs make honey, and we eat it the supply ourselves. On Earth, your Bees are the only animals that make food for humans, fresh honey."

Bill started to open to me about his incredible story. He spoke of Centaurs, creatures from another world. I felt like I was a part of some sci-fi movie, but then reality hit me.

"Our planet has diversity in "top human," he continued, "bottom insect/animal" and "top insect/animal bottom human." We need to somehow focus our strengths on agricultural education, understanding that we only have the same basic tools as your earth cave dwellers made and used. My job here on Earth is to either gather physical seeds or agricultural education that would adapt to our planet's trees, plants, foliage, soil, and available tools. Your scientific community has learned a great deal about the effects of the space environment on seed germination, metabolism, genetics, biochemistry, and even seed production, but my need would be to transport those seeds or valuable information to Pherzon and see if they can adapt to our planet."

As I listened to Bill's explanation, I could not believe what I was hearing. This was all so incredible, but at the same time, it made sense. The Centaurs had come to Earth to seek out knowledge and bring it back to their planet. When Bill finished speaking, I was stunned once again. So, the alien abductions were not some cruel experiment or strange fascination but rather an effort to improve the future of Pherzon.

"But what about those who claim to have been abducted against their will?" I pressed, still trying to wrap my head around the concept.

Bill's expression became more serious. "There are those among us who are more aggressive in their approach. Who do not share our beliefs and methods," he admitted. "They take humans without our consent, and we cannot condone their actions. They believe that taking humans without their consent is necessary for our survival. We are doing everything in our power to stop them, but they are a small group, and they are difficult to track down."

I could see the pain in Bill's eyes as he spoke, and I knew that this was not an easy topic for him. Though, my heart sank at the thought of innocent people being taken from their lives without warning. "Do they harm them?" I asked, my voice shaking.

Bill shook his head. "No, we do not harm humans," he said firmly. "But we understand that it can be a traumatic experience for them, which is why we only take those who we believe will be willing to help us."

I could not help but feel conflicted about all of this. On the one hand, the Centaurs were seeking out knowledge for the betterment of their own society, but on the other hand, they were taking humans without their consent. I knew I needed to think about this more before making any decisions.

"But why didn't you tell me all of this from the beginning?" I asked, feeling a bit hurt that he had kept such a massive secret from me.

"I didn't know if I could trust you," he admitted. "And I still don't know if I can fully trust you. But I needed to tell someone, and you were the only one who seemed open-minded enough to believe me."

I nodded, feeling a sense of understanding wash over me. This was a lot to take in, but I knew that I was in it for the long haul.

"Instead of abducting people, why don't you invite them?" I asked Bill.

"Inviting is not an option. I do not think the human would willingly come. As I and my workers and drones can morph into a new unknown human form, the Queen can also "take over" a human's existing body. We make sure our person of choice has selected a vacation of sorts on Earth so there is no suspicion as to their whereabouts. We are also involved in the planning of their vacation or desertion details. At the right time, in the dark of night, the Queen enters and takes over the human body. Along with two of her resolute drones, we travel back to Pherzon, where the Queen will lay the human body down in soft grass to recover, and it is then the Queen leaves the body. The possession takes the strength out of the human, so we care for the human in a morphed human form until they recover, so when they "come to, "they recognize a human form. Then, as I talked to you about Centaurs and Pherzon, we slowly tell our story and let the human know where he or she is, why they are here, and if they cooperate, will travel back to Earth. As we seem odd looking to earthlings, we are also friendly, and our visitors

27

always agree, overwhelmed at the opportunity of helping. Over the past 30 years, we have gained valuable information from these encounters. When the schooling is complete, we thank our visitors and tell them to get a good night's sleep for their journey back, and through the night, a Queen will take over the body again, and when the human awakes, they are home from vacation. Of course, the human remembers nothing from the event, but as we have seen, the human brain does display memories of the experience as time goes on.

As Bill spoke, my body seemed to freeze, and I felt as if all the energy had been drained from me. A part of me wanted to run, to escape from this unbelievable story, but another part was curious, eager to know more.

Bill's voice continued to fill the surroundings, painting a picture of a world that was beyond anything I had ever imagined. Every word he spoke was like a puzzle piece, fitting perfectly into the grand story he was telling.

Despite my fear, I could not help but be captivated by his tale, hanging on to every word he said. There was something in the way he spoke that made it all seem real as if he genuinely believed every word he was saying.

"Hence, an alien abduction, which again has no verification, and your media uses it to add to the Alien frenzy. Sometimes our abducted human will add to the story and believe the added additions themselves, which even makes the story juicier or crazy, depending on who is listening. I sat there frozen. It all made too much sense. It all fits. It sounded crazy but it all fit! What was I to do? I felt like I was in an episode of ALF. I was a friend of an Alien living on Earth, but with a Catch-22, but just like the show ALF, I could not tell anyone. They would put me in a stray jacket, and I would just be another Alien sighting story. How ironic. They did have it all figured out. It was a perfect storm for the centaurs!"

CHAPTER 5

I was stunned by Bill's revelation, unable to comprehend the gravity of his words. I had always believed that the existence of extraterrestrial life was a mere fantasy, a figment of our imagination. But here I was, standing face to face with an alien from the planet Pherzon, whose mission was to gather knowledge and resources to sustain his planet.

As I processed this information, I couldn't help but ask, "How long have you been on Earth, Bill?"

"I have been here for over three Earth decades," he replied. "Our mission is not a short one, and we cannot leave until we have achieved our goals."

I was intrigued by his response and probed further, "How do you decide which hive to reside in?"

Bill explained, "We monitor the progress of different hives and determine which one shows the most promise. At present, Washington, DC, is the most promising hive, particularly because of the Department of Agriculture's research on Nanotechnology. My role has been to oversee the 'seeds for the Future' program, which they believe is for Earth's population. But, in reality, it is to gather knowledge to sustain our planet."

I was amazed at the extent of their mission and asked, "Do all Centaurs live in human form on Earth?"

Bill replied, "Yes, we all live in human form to mask our identity. We have apartments to complete our human being montage, but we do not eat or sleep in them. We live by our functions when we are in bee form, which is why we do not eat in human form and sleep wherever we find comfort outside."

I could not fathom the level of commitment and dedication required to fulfill their mission. "This is such an important mission for your planet. What will happen once your mission is complete?" I asked.

Bill responded, "Once our planet has enough healthy food to sustain our population, along with education and tools to sustain it, we will return home. Our goal is the survival and prosperity of our planet, and we will do anything to achieve it."

I was in awe of Bill's dedication and commitment to his mission, but I couldn't help but feel conflicted. On the one hand, I admired their mission and the lengths they were willing to go to achieve it, but on the other hand, I could not help but worry about the impact it would have on Earth and its inhabitants.

As I continued to ponder these thoughts, Bill's final words echoed in my mind, "Other than your passion for Aliens and UFOs, which ironically fuels our mask."

Again, I was astonished, and I knew the amazement would only grow through time. I needed to play this information by ear, day to day, not telling anyone but also not being awkward around Bill. I had information that the CIA or the President of the United States did not have or was I just assuming that.

As the conversation ended, Bill turned to me with a serious expression. "I need to know, are we still friends?" he asked.

I paused, unsure of how to respond. "I don't really have a choice," I finally said with a smile. "If I say I'm not your friend, I know what my fate would be."

Bill nodded, understanding the weight of the situation. "Then I'll have to judge for myself if you're still trustworthy and if we're still friending as if none of this information had been shared," he said.

We both knew that the night had changed the course of our relationship forever.

"Let's call it a night, friend," Bill said before we parted ways.

As I walked away, my thoughts were in a frenzy, unsure if my newfound knowledge was a blessing or a curse.

As the days went on, Bill and I became more than just acquaintances. Our conversations grew more comfortable, and I was eager to learn more about his time on Earth and his plans. Bill spoke of his invaluable work with Agricultural humans, teaching the Centaurs how to farm better, conserve resources, and use natural medicine. He spoke about how every Centaur had a unique form for different tasks, and he was on a new mission to save Earth's Queen Bees from their destructive fate.

"When Earth Bees choose their Queen Bee," Bill explained, "there is a fight to the death to destroy other future Queen Bees. We are saving those Queen Bees and stunning them for their travel to Pherzon. One hundred Queen Bees per trip scattered throughout Planet Pherzon would mean millions of new visitors and hives. Our Bee Centaurs create and consume their own honey, but they would love to share the honey with the balance of our planet. It is a win for Pherzon."

Bill continued, "Insect pollinators, including honeybees, co-evolved with flowering plants over millions of years. Plants developed floral parts with increasingly specialized features to attract visiting insects who would, in turn, distribute pollen grains and optimize the plant's reproductive capabilities. These wasp-like insects underwent physiological changes to take advantage of the nutritional benefits offered by flowering plants."

He added, "If we can take advantage of Earth Bees in large numbers spread throughout planet Pherzon, it will absolutely help our system, even change it for the better. Your Earth Bees seem to adapt as well or better on Pherzon due to it being a virgin planet with no factories or cars, only natural pollution. They also took to the 'pecking order' and never even bothered any other centaurs, as the centaurs knew to live in harmony with their smaller but helpful neighbors."

He added, "All our 'Hives' on Earth are searching for insects, pollinators. They are integral to a healthy environment and the planet's survival. Bill continued that his own studies show that bees are the most important species on earth.

As I grew more fascinated by Bill's work on Pherzon, I could not resist the urge to learn more. I asked him if we could meet up on the weekend, hoping to glean some insight into his world. But to my surprise, he told me that on weekends, he and his team transformed into bees and headed back to their planet for some rest and updates. But Bill, ever the gracious host, suggested we spend a Saturday together at the Smithsonian National Zoological Park. I jumped at the chance to catch up with him.

That next Saturday Morning, we met. I assumed he spent the night at the zoo. We met as we always do, on a bench outside of a trail.

"Good morning, Bill," I said, "How was your night?"

"Excellent," he replied.

"It is a strange little meeting outside of work," I said. Though as excited as I was with my newly founded Sci-Fi information. "I would like to have all my questions answered so I can feel more comfortable with you," I added.

"I understand," replied Bill. "My biggest question is that you have been on Earth for so long, when is your mission completed?"

"Well, since we first started occupying Earth, we are now down to about one-quarter of the centaurs we started with. Science in the field of Agriculture is nowhere near its peak, so I can safely say we will just leave a handful of centaurs in each of our Earth hives. Our biggest fear," Bill continued, "is to have a Centaur captured. Our Queen, workers, and drone centaurs know what they must do if there is a capture. That is not the problem. Our quandary is for someone to just know that we are here on Earth and then question where we came from. Whether it would be the USA or an International Community that finds us, I know that in the end, they would want to use our capability for war and our planet to reduce Earth's climate change. They would understand that we could be a much greater fighter than any of their special op's military. Any leader would know that we could appear from nowhere and strike without warning and be back on the soil before anyone knew anything that happened. We would be deadlier than any drone that anyone could manufacture, but that is not what our nature is, and we would never engage in that type of behavior. Keeping our planet Pherzon a secret is just as important as keeping our mission secret. You are the only known human that knows our whereabouts on Earth and our mission to support our planet."

I looked at him and silently listened to what he was saying.

After a brief pause, he said, "My trust in your secrecy has approval throughout all our hives on Earth. It is the first in Centaur history. It was always imperative that we have communication with a human, but the partnership needed to be non-partisan with trust, and that is why we chose you. The longer we stay on Earth, it is inevitable that we will get involved in Earth's matters," continued Bill. "On Pherzon, the Queen Bee is the only Centaur that can kill. The Queen is a Judge and Jury. On Earth, sometimes the Queen cannot ignore what they see. Throughout the Hives on Earth, our Queens tend to live in the parks when they are not in human form. Living in parks for years, you tend to see shocking behavior from humans, behavior not accepted on Pherzon. As a Queen myself, I have dealt with such behavior swiftly, trying not to alarm the victim but bringing swift action and the disappearance of the accomplice. I am sure our actions throughout our hives on Earth add to your missing person's rank. It was not what we intended to do when we visited, but it had become a result. We have also been involved in Earth's highest profile missing person cases, but not by choice. On Pherzon, when you abuse a being, you deal with the consequence. If I or one of my centaurs happens to be in the same area and witnesses a victim of abuse on Earth, we do not acknowledge fame, faces, or names. We deal with the abuser as quickly as we can without notice. It is our nature. Our hives have dealt with poachers in Africa to the destruction of the Amazon rainforest. Supplying ourselves with nutrition was our mission, but seeing wrong while being there was addressed swiftly, but it cannot be our eternal fight. It must be the USA's."

As Bill was talking, my mind was racing through missing person cases like Jimmy Hoffa and wondering if it was possible these Centaurs were involved.

CHAPTER 6

As the weeks went by, Bill and I continued our discussions about his mission for Pherzon and how it related to his personal life on Earth. He emphasized that any action on Earth was not the mission's main objective, but they did not have specific actions that could be helpful. Bill explained that the Queen Centaur was the only member of the hive that stayed until replaced from their age or an unethical decision was made on their part. The worker and drone force schedules rotated due to their work ethic, and they made interplanetary travel to update messages and share their success on their mission.

"To fully energize these workers," Bill said, "we have a rotation to the Amazon Rainforest where they can feast on different kinds of honey for a full week and store enough for Pherzon."

"In the rainforest, they can feast on their choice of honey and still stay away from any human interaction. The existing bee population accepts them, and they educate themselves on their honey process and which honeys have medicinal properties for those on Pherzon," Bill continued. He listed the diverse types of honey in the rainforest, including Acacia, Manuka, Alfalfa, Avocado, Blueberry, Eucalyptus, Clover, Sage, Orange Blossom, and Pine Tree Honey. He also mentioned that this was a favorite spot for Queen

Centaurs to educate themselves on the plentiful foliage, which was the nucleus of their mission.

"However, due to our high profile in the Rainforest, there have been UFO sightings in the area, which we are trying to control," Bill added.

As Bill shared his information, I felt like I was piecing together a puzzle about UFOs. Memories of stories on UFO sightings fit perfectly together with the information he was giving me. It was mind-blowing.

Overwhelmed by the information, I told Bill I needed to go home early and rest. I felt like I had just stumbled upon a best-selling nonfiction story.

"You have a nonfiction story that could be a bestseller," I told him.

Bill laughed and agreed, "Let's take a break and rest up."

As I walked away, my emotions were all over the place. I felt so entitled. "Why me? Why do I have this information?" I felt both excited and scared, like Mike Myers in a horror movie. I could not believe I was privy to this information. It was like being Alfred the Butler, knowing the secret identities of Batman and Robin. My head was spinning as I had just consumed five Red Bulls, and I desperately needed to rest my mind. So, I decided to go home, have a nightcap, and sleep through the night.

CHAPTER 7

The next morning, I woke up feeling refreshed and ready to tackle the day. As I started brewing my coffee, I turned on the news and was immediately hit with a shocking story: two of the top Generals in Russia had gone missing overnight. I could not take my eyes off the television as the coverage continued, explaining that there was no evidence of their whereabouts and no leads. Russian intelligence had no information, and Putin was quick to point the finger at the United States. Our relationship with Russia was already on thin ice, and this news only made it worse. Our President had to assure Putin that we were not involved in any way.

At work that day, everyone was buzzing with questions and meetings. The news of the Russian Generals' disappearance had shaken everyone, and we were all on edge. And then, the next night, tragedy struck again: two top Generals in North Korea went missing without a trace. The United States was again suspected, and every country was on high alert, waiting for the next move.

The tension was palpable as everyone waited to see if the abductions would continue. Fortunately, the next night was quiet, but the relief was short-lived. The following morning, news broke that a top general from China had been abducted, and this time there was a photo. The photo showed a guard dog barking at a figure tampering with a camera, a face familiar to me that took me to my knees, the figure of a glowing alien face.

The situation was unbelievable. No one knew what was happening or why, and every country was on high alert. It was like something out of a science fiction movie, but I knew better.

China questioned if the release of the photo was a joke intended to embarrass them if it was a copycat venture and if the Chinese General was missing. China refused to release the actual photo to the governments, fearing that it would make them a laughingstock among other countries. Despite a week of investigation that yielded no leads, Russia, and North Korea pressured China to release the photo to the Governments, who were then given the option of showing their own civilians. As a person in a high-clearance government position, I had access to the photo. During the unveiling of the photo, as it was passed around the table, my heart started to flutter. I tried to remain calm and blend in with the emotions around the table, but reactions like "Is this a joke?" and "Why are we even wasting a meeting on this?" made me realize that something was off. So, I excused myself from the meeting and immediately went to find Bill.

The picture I saw in the meeting was the same one I had seen in the park when I was looking for Bill. There was no mistake. This photo caught on camera in China was either Bill or one of his drones. "But why? What had happened so quickly?" Questions started pouring into my mind that I needed answers to.

What if Bill had already seen the photo and was waiting for me? I opened his office door, and greeted him with a "Good Morning, Bill. Can we talk?"

He responded, "Absolutely. It's a beautiful morning. Let's walk to the park."

As we walked, I sensed that something was off. We arrived at the park, where everything had started. I asked Bill if the photo was of him or one of his drones.

He remained quiet as we walked further, and then he finally spoke, saying, "They knew about me."

The CIA had been following him for months on a tip, recording his transformations and more. They were unsure of what to do about him for fear of a war with his drones.

"As I explained my reasons for being on Earth, the CIA made a promise: my planet would never run out of food or medicine if we stood beside the USA," said Bill.

I couldn't believe it. The scenario I constantly worried about had happened. What was I to do? So, I created an international scene to take the blame from me. "Bill, do they know about me?" I asked as we walked. Bill turned into the area where he fed the bee honey. "Do they know about you?" he replied. "I was going to ask you the same thing."

A split second later, I felt a sting in my chest. I was staring at Bill in bee form. I was in shock, my head tilted down looking at a stinger which pierced my heart right through my back. Bill replied, "You were the snitch."

I shook my head. "No," still in shock, as he pulled his stinger from my body ever so slowly, and I could feel and hear flesh popping. I could hear buzzing, my eyes opened in panic, and tears ran down my face. I lay there stunned, still hearing buzzing. I was staring at a familiar sight.

I sat up frantically in fear, slowly looking around and then realizing I was in my bedroom and my alarm clock was buzzing. Oh my God, it was a dream, no, a nightmare. I jumped up and turned on the TV, checked my phone for alerts and trends. It was a dream, an unbelievable 'I swore it was real' dream. I felt my heart and laid back in bed. It was a strong drink I had taken to fall asleep.

I went to work that morning, knowing I would never forget that dream and realizing how delicate this situation was in which I was involved. I needed to make peace with myself. No more nightmares. I knew what I had to do. I needed closure to the information I had. I felt as if I had the nuclear code. I was going to ask Bill if he could take me to Pherzon. I thought if I could see the planet, my mind would be at peace.

I finally found time with Bill and told him about my dream.

"It was so real, I sprung out of bed sweating in fear," I told him.

Bill replied, "If seeing my planet will give you closure, then I am for it." He continued, "Tell me what night and when you are sound asleep. I will take your body to Pherzon."

"Please give me a few days to prepare myself," I replied.

I knew what I had to do. I scheduled a vacation and updated my notes up until the night of the body transfer just in case I did not return to Earth. If I went missing, my lawyer would know where to find the book, and they could decide whether I was credible or simply crazy.

The next day, I set the 'body transfer' for that night. I was ready. Bill explained that people typically do not know when they are ready for possession, which makes it easy for them to take over their bodies while they are sound asleep and, in a limp, REM state. However, since I knew he was coming, the anticipation of the takeover might keep me awake, and the transfer might not work. I assured him that it would.

That night, I went home and drank exactly what I had when I had my nightmare: fresh moonshine.

CHAPTER 8

I woke up the next morning and thought, "It did not work. I'm in another dream."

But Bill was by my side. Why was I laying down, nude in the grass? Wow, that moonshine is special. Bill was not talking. I slowly looked around, feeling as if I was in Jurassic Park. My eyes were catching up to the motion of my body. I was sitting in pure Utopia. The only thing I could hear was the rustling wind over the grass and animal sounds.

"You made it," Bill whispered, "Welcome to Pherzon."

I slowly sat up, feeling as if I had run a marathon. But why was I tired? Bill did all the work. "Why am I so weak?" I asked.

"The transfer takes a huge amount of energy from both of us," Bill explained. "Give it an hour, and we will be walking around together. In the meantime, drink this juice. Do you mind if I take my real form?" Bill asked. "You've been through much, and I don't want to freak you out."

"Feel natural and comfortable," I replied.

Within a second of my answer, Bill was in Bee form, always shocking, and I couldn't imagine being calm at the look, but I had a feeling I was set to see so much more. It was so peaceful here, and what was I drinking? It tasted like the nectar of the gods.

"All natural, all nutrition for your system to Gas Up," Bill replied.

"I'm feeling better. Can I try to stand now?" I asked.

"Let's see those sea legs," Bill replied.

I felt like a fawn trying to stand with my mother's help, but there I was, standing and witnessing beautiful acres of land. I was in awe. I understood already why Pherzon was so important to Bill. No buildings, no smokestacks, no cars. I could see no carbon footprint. As we walked further, I saw fresh green grass, brown rich dirt, blue clear water, and northern light shaded skies.

"I just wondered if the earth ever appreciated its surroundings before the Industrial Revolution," I said. "I guess we must learn from mistakes first to appreciate what we have lost."

We continued walking slowly.

"You are doing great," said Bill.

As we grew closer to some movement up ahead, I watched with astonishment. We slowly walked by half horse half human centaurs, not at all shocked to see me due to being friendly with the Queen. The further we walked, the more I was amazed. If you walked the acres of land in Africa, from horses to zebras to Lions, there was a centaur here to match it. Somehow in the beginning stages of Pherzon, there were creatures with this ability, and through generations of evolution, they grew into Centaur beings. It was truly an amazing sight. You could see why Bill was worried about the food supply.

As we continued to walk, I was amazed at the organization of the planet. Perfect rows and rows of trees and plants in open areas were planted. Structures on the planet were built strongly from wood and forest material. I wondered how they were able to do this. It was not long before I found out. Ahead of us were humans, and I stopped and looked at Bill as if I were part of a prison movie.

"What is going on, Bill?" I asked. "I thought you brought humans here for their educational skills and then took them back home."

"That is true," answered Bill. "But every human you see chose to stay here. When we found Earth, we knew immediately that this was our 'perfect storm.' Humans have the mobility and the hands for mechanical work, and our centaurs have great strength. For years we would select humans with 'no baggage,' basic loners, young and strong. We use the same tactic as your armed forces, look to give their lives meaning, a belonging, a family. We would handpick humans for the skills we needed on Pherzon, and it worked. Once they woke up here and realized it was no dream, they were here to stay. These humans have families, and their children now collaborate with our centaurs. It worked out better than we could have imagined. We became a stronger family than we ever were before. Everyone now has a purpose."

I looked at Bill hesitantly and said, "Is that why I am here? Did you know at some point in time that you would bring me here?"

"I did," Bill answered. "I knew just from you being inquisitive you would want to see the planet I constantly talked about. No worries, though. You may leave tonight if you like. You are not one of our recruiters, but you are welcome to stay."

Believe me, it is so tranquil, so inviting, and so friendly that I thought about it.

CHAPTER 9

I spent weeks getting to know the planet. It was amazing how the humans and centaurs worked together. The horse and zebra centaurs let the family's children ride on them. At night, I would sit with the humans and talk to them about how they ended up on Pherzon. All of them were mentally damaged on Earth, but when they found Pherzon, it gave them meaning, a reason to live. On this planet, there was no need for money or status; everyone worked to keep the planet healthy so the planet could keep them healthy. It was like a neighborhood on Earth where everyone knew each other, with no locked doors or closed car windows. People didn't look behind their backs because everyone was looking out for each other.

I was enjoying my stay so much that I felt like I was on the best vacation of my life, but I knew it was time to go home. I searched for Bill and finally found him.

"Welcome," he said. "How is your stay so far? I have heard good things."

"It's pure heaven here," I replied. "I now know why you want to protect it, but I must hesitantly say, 'I must go home.'"

Bill looked at me and said, "Houston, we have a problem," and laughed.

My facial expression dropped. "What do you mean?" I asked slowly.

"My duties as a queen in an Earth hive have changed," he explained. "I have a replacement due to my number of missions and body takeovers. It takes a toll on your stamina. My replacement is already on Earth, performing my duties as Bill. That is why you have not seen me. Diversity takes a while to exchange information and human morphing identification. I talked to my replacement queen, and she was not one to 'take over' a human body and transfer it to Earth. Please be assured, I am working on the situation and will find a solution."

With a worried look, I confirmed Bill's statement. My worry, I thought to myself, was that I had talked to my lawyer before I left and told him that if I did not return before three weeks, to give my notes to the two designated people written on the front of the envelope. I was on the cusp of three weeks, wondering if I should say anything to Bill. This was exactly what I had tried to leave Earth from, but it had followed me. Bill would be so upset that I had even had notes and set this up, but he needed to understand that I was worried about Earth, just as he was worried about Pherzon. If I did not tell him, my notes would go to Joe and Nancy, and I did not know how they would react to them. If they thought there was something to my notes, they had the power to react, and the existing centaurs would indeed have exposure, eventually by the FBI or CIA. This could be happening already as I continued my notes on Pherzon. I needed to tell Bill, even though I knew my death could be the outcome.

I walked the area and watched the humans collaborating with the Centaurs. The planet was amazing, a throwback to the days before the Industrial Revolution. If Earth set up surveillance and found these centaurs, the next stop would be Pherzon. I could not let that happen.

I searched for Bill and found him landing from a trip around the planet. The Queens of Pherzon would make sure the planet was always safe and ready for planting or habitation. Bill witnessed me in the brush and coasted over.

"Hello, stranger, how are we doing?" He spoke.

"I'm not doing well," I said. "But first, I'd like to know your Pherzon name."

"My name is Apus," she responded.

I reminded her of the shock I felt when I first met her, seeing her feeding in the park and being knocked down by her defense glow. Apus tilted her head, and I couldn't read her expression. I told her about my journal and how I had designated two people to receive it in case I did not return from Earth in three weeks. I assured her that I had never intended to use it, but I needed a backup plan just in case. I also knew that the centaurs had their own backup plan if things went wrong on Earth.

"If the FBI and CIA are involved with your notes, our backup plan will be initiated," Apus said. "There is no telling how far this might reach. I will need to send drones back to the hives with this information to prepare 'Bill,' who has taken over the Washington hive. He will be the one making the future decisions. I am afraid neither you nor I will have a good outcome after this."

With that, Apus went to round up drones to carry the information to the active hives on Earth. Until we had updates from Earth, I was sure it was going to be tense between Apus and myself. We were both in the same Catch-22.

CHAPTER 10

Weeks went by, and Apus suggested that I collaborate with the humans in any way that would be helpful. The humans did not judge me; they understood that I had love for Pherzon and Earth, but the outcome of what was done could be deadly. I wondered what kind of "meeting" could be held peacefully if surveillance had been started, and who would benefit. There was always a workload scheduled on the planet to keep it organized. It was always a hard day's work, but you prospered at night knowing it was being done for us and our family.

One cool morning, I awoke to start my day's work only to be shocked by what I saw outside. Joe and Nancy were lying in a bed of grass, brought to Pherzon for reasons unknown. Centaurs stood over them in human form, so as not to shock them when they awoke. I could only assume that Bill, Joe, and Nancy were now morphed Bee Centaurs, but I didn't ask why. It was clear that the centaurs were skilled at this transformation, even with the high security on both Joe and Nancy.

I knew I couldn't stare or hover in the area, as I was the reason they were here, and I didn't want to raise any questions. I prepared myself for work and when I returned, they were nowhere to be found. Apus would stop by to check on us, but it was like we were just acquaintances now. I knew there was a plan in the works, but I was left completely in the dark. Despite this, I was grateful to be alive and living on such a beautiful planet with friendly people and centaurs. I was getting used to the work during the day and the family time and conversations at night. There were no televisions, phones, or computers, only storytelling and enjoyable conversation.

The next morning, I woke up in my own bed on Earth in Washington DC. I wondered how the centaurs felt about me and what I had done. My answer came in the form of being sent back to Earth.

"What do I do now?" I wondered aloud to myself. I checked the news from the past three weeks and found that nothing crazy had happened. Then, I frantically searched for my notes, but could not find them. Finally, I decided to contact my lawyer, but to my surprise, his office was now occupied by a doctor's practice.

It felt like my life was back to where it was the day before I witnessed Bill in the park as an alien. But my mind was still fresh with what I had seen and known about the centaurs. I am more confused now than ever before. Why did they bring me back? Were Bill, Joe, and Nancy morphed centaurs now? And if so, where were their human forms? Was there a plan to take over Earth? Were the hives still active here and internationally? Were they waiting for me to self-destruct? I could not go through this again. I had to try to ignore it all and keep my head on a swivel to see what would happen next.

With a heavy heart, I called work and told them that I had been sick and needed more time before coming back to work. Without hesitation, they granted me sick time.

CHAPTER 11

In the next few weeks, I decided to rewrite my notes, compiling them from when I met Bill until now, without really knowing why. I needed to calm down and stop worrying about everything. My appetite had changed, and I did not feel like myself. I needed to get out and take a walk. I went to my favorite park, the one that had started my terrible roller coaster ride. People looked different to me, and I seemed to hear and smell things I had never noticed before. Maybe it was just me trying to be calm, to ignore the past couple of weeks. As I walked by people, I stared into their eyes, and it was creeping them out. I walked by a woman with a spiral glare in her eyes. That was it; I was scheduling a doctor's appointment.

As I walked further, I saw the same woman with the spiral glare. I tried to look away, but before I could, she stopped and spoke to me. "Good morning," she said. "Would you like to sit and talk?"

"No, thank you," I responded.

"Don't you just love the smell of flowers?" She said, laughing.

"Pardon me?" I responded.

"Don't you just love the smell of flowers?" She repeated.

"Yes, I do," I said, taking a deep breath. "It's nature's calming effect."

"Funny, though," she said. "There are no flowers around here but for those one hundred feet away." I looked around and then stared at her in confusion. As people passed by, there were nothing but dead eyes. But when I looked into her eyes, that spiral glare was prominent.

"Would you like to sit down?" She asked.

I knew I was digging a deeper, more complex hole by saying, "Yes, I would."

"My name is Audrey, and you do not need to see a doctor," she said.

I froze. I knew it. This was the amusement park ride that would never end.

"You wanted to get off so badly, but all you could do was hold on. You wanted to know why we brought you back. I am here to tell you. We need humans to interact with. We need to know their opinions. Their history on earth is important to us. It is not biased. But as we have found, humans end up loyal to earth, which is also a trait we like. If you are loyal to Earth, then you can be loyal to Pherzon. This is the reason your appetite, olfactory, and audio senses feel different. While you were on Pherzon, we cleared a path for you on Earth. While you were with the humans on Pherzon, half of the bee centaur capability was transferred to you, as was also done to me. You have the Centaur senses and family traits but do not have their form. To put it lightly, you are now what earthlings term an alien, but Centaurs have names for us. We are Bisects. Making you and me family, Centaurs can now trust us. What you need to know now is that there is a family, or hive, of Bisects on Earth. We are like a 'test tube' centaur. As such, we are not like Centaurs and not like humans. I am here to give you information on how you must manage yourself now."

I looked at Audrey with utter confusion, not sure how to respond to the information she was providing me with.

"Bisects have their own Physicians and overall healthcare. Bisects immediately identify other Bisects and Morphed Bee to humans, just as you identified me by my eyes," Audrey continued.

"But how?" I interrupted. "How did they give me their DNA, so to speak?"

"While you slept with the humans on Pherzon, a queen inserted her stinger from the back, behind your heart, and injected your system," Audrey explained. "The initial sting puts you in a comatose state. It goes in deep enough but away from the heart and then pulls out to leave a healing scab. Of course, you cannot see it because it is on your back, but we call it our 'bimark,' as you would call your 'birthmark.' The mark heals itself to a quarter-inch perfect hole and is another way to identify Bisects."

Audrey handed me a paper. "Familiarize yourself with this. It is an instruction sheet for the dark web. Information is there for all Bisects: the 'what, where, and how of a

Bisects survival.' Soon enough, you will meet with other Bisects who will also help you out with their own experiences."

I looked at the paper and just could not believe what I was seeing. There was a whole other world that existed on Earth, and humans were intrigued by the idea, the idea of aliens.

I sat there in disbelief, feeling like it was the same day I witnessed Bill exposed as a Centaur.

"When would this runaway train slow down?" I thought to myself.

Audrey could sense my fear, and whispered, "Slow down. No fears. That is plenty for the day."

I looked at her in question and asked, "What do I do now?"

Audrey replied, "Nothing. Take another two weeks off from work, and all the information you will need will come to you. The only thing we ask is that you keep a low profile. You will come to know your mission just as the thousands of other bisects here on earth have. You are another of 'the chosen.' They see you as too important to the future of Pherzon to silence, so they made you a part of the circle that makes up our Bisects, Morphed Centaurs, and Transporters that will keep Pherzon alive and thriving forever."

I stood up in fear and stared at Audrey, feeling like a double agent. I was scared.

"I need to leave," I said. "Thank you for the information."

I walked away in a daze, wanting to go home and feel safe while thinking about everything. I cut across the park for the shortest distance to my house. Even though I was flustered with questions running through my mind, I sensed someone following me. Without turning around, I sensed his figure, intention, and distance which was growing closer. I turned toward him with only inches between us, and it all seemed like slow motion. As the assailant swung at the side of my face, I stopped his hand and firmly threw him to the ground. I stood over him in confidence as he lay there with a terrified look on his face, staring into my eyes. He crept backwards in fright and jumped to his feet, looking back as he ran back to the park trail.

It was amazing, it felt like I had enough time to do anything, I felt strong and secure, no fear. I looked around to see if anyone had noticed, but we were too far off the trail, which is why he planned his attack. I felt like Superman, standing there still taking it all in. My life had changed, again.

I started thinking about feeling safe again and headed home. Once I entered my home, I felt as if my life was normal. I did as I normally do, put on some coffee, sat on the couch, and grabbed the remote. I sat there looking at the paper Audrey had handed me. This was all real, it was not going away. I knew I must make peace with myself and accept my future. I must admit, now I was already thinking about how I would be looking at people in Washington. Who will I see as a Bisect and, God forbid, who will I see as a Morphed human? It always made me wonder, where are their bodies and why weren't they chosen as Bisects? Of course, I knew this was much bigger than Washington, this could be worldwide. I felt as if I was under one of those protection programs, ready to resurface in a week or so. I needed this time at home to take it all in and slowly accept the next chapter of my life.

CHAPTER 12

Reluctantly, I finally made my way back to work with my new identity. For the first few days, I would overfocus to see who was human and who was not. I did not want to be seen as shady. By the end of the month, I had a clear picture. The Centaurs had chosen the USA for the heartbeat of Pherzon. They knew they could rely on us for technology and future longevity. They had hives placed strategically in international countries to make sure the USA had a dominant position in all matters. The Centaurs used the Earth like a chessboard, guarding their greatest asset, the USA.

As time passed, I became more comfortable with my new identity. One day, as I was leaving work, I noticed a man following me. He had a strange look on his face, and it made me uneasy. I decided to take a detour to my car, but the man continued to follow me. Finally, I turned around and asked, "Can I help you?"

The man replied, "Sorry, I did not mean to startle you. I just wanted to ask if you are a Bisect?"

Even though we had identified ourselves already by instinct, I paused for a moment, unsure of how to respond. Finally, I replied, "Yes, I am."

The man's face lit up with excitement, "Me too! It is great to meet another one of us."

We exchanged information and talked about our experiences as Bisects. It was a relief to know that I was not alone in this new world. As I drove home, I realized that my life had changed once again, but this time it was for the better.

Some of the people I had worked with, and my acquaintances were morphed and now looked at me differently. It was an exchange of communication I could not explain, like we were Masons who secretly identified with each other. My thoughts were now consumed by questions like "where are their human bodies," and "will they ever be transferred back again?" I prayed no real harm came to them.

It was a perfect storm for the Pherzon Centaurs. They needed our constantly updated technology, and they could control what and how to receive it. Their speed, power, and morphing capabilities were used for ingenuity, not war. Due to confusion between Centaur sightings and alien sightings, they were cloaked from human interest. They were like Big Foot - a mystery that caused excitement, not fear, since people knew nothing about them except for their "sightings." It was a perfect storm for interesting and intuitive media spots, a conversation.

My focus shifted to the government. Who knew about the Centaurs? Who allowed these sightings to continue as mysterious alien sightings? Who turned these sightings, since the 1950s, into unknown or dismissed sightings? Who was the first to speak with a Bee Centaur and say "Yes," we will work perfectly together? The deal was the USA would ensure a plentiful and thriving Pherzon, and Centaurs would give the USA an "edge" in being number one in the world with their strategically placed hives.

Since I was now part of Pherzon as a Bisect, I knew they could keep in constant communication with me. However, my plan now was to find out how deep Pherzon was in our government, and if the Centaurs could be manipulated to serve as soldiers against our enemies, a power one hundred times greater than any special operation force.

The End

About The Author

Greetings,

I am James C. Reinhold, Author.

I happily retired after 30 years of service doing something I loved doing. My passion now is to write engaging, science fiction, fantasy, and religious stories. I enjoy writing, as I am a new and enthusiastic author with a vision for fiction. My hope is to have my stories earn readers. This time, I have decided to collect all my work in one place, and let your imagination select your journey. Fantasy, Fiction, and Religion are my genres at present.

Books Driven by Passion

Reading is a personal journey. Bookmark your next reading journey with us. Select books that embrace your imagination at our cozy site and experience reading like you are in the story. All my books are Journeys that hopefully never lose your interest as readers, each of my books will embrace your imagination, from visiting Christmas 1967 to traveling through wormholes. As you start to read my books, you feel gripped by the storyline. Before putting my thoughts to the pen, I consider the story from every aspect to ensure that my readers have something interesting to read, like suddenly hearing that favorite song that just came on the radio, Turn it Up!

A Book for Every Taste @ ReadtoRelax.com

At Readtorelax.com

Our Family Friendly Bookstore offers;
 Neverending Stories including a Hallmark style
Christmas Classic
 No AI writing
   Enjoy your visit to our "Cozy Getaway."

ReadtoRelax.com

Bring your Imagination and Relax with a book from our interesting selection, then browse Childhood Memories throughout our website.

James C. Reinhold